The Ballet School stood halfway along Onion Avenue. Morris went nervously inside and found a door marked

MADAME BUTTERFLY

He pushed open the door. Madame Butterfly lay on a sofa dressed in flowing silks of red and blue and yellow.

'I'd like to join your ballet class,' said Morris timidly.

'Well!' she said. 'A millipede in a ballet class! Whatever next!'

Books published by Red Fox in the Read Alone series

The Trouble with Herbert
Herbert Saves the Day
Stinky Cynthia
by Heather Eyles

Trouble Next Door
Philomena Hall and the Great Gerbil Caper
by Roy Apps

Henry's Most Unusual Birthday
by Elizabeth Hawkins

My Kid Sister
by E. W. Hildick

Cat's Witch
Cat's Witch and the Monster
Cat's Witch and the Wizard
by Kara May

I Want to be on TV
by Penny Speller

The Great Blackpool Sneezing Attack
by Barbara Mitchelhill

Stanley Makes it Big
by John Talbot

Blue Magic
Amos Shrike, the School Ghost
Snakes Alive!
Through the Witch's Window
by Hazel Townson

Lily and Lorna
The Salt and Pepper Boys
The Pop Concert
by Jean Wills

Rolf and Rosie
by Robert Swindells

Wilfred's Wolf
by Jenny Nimmo

Cabbages from Outer Space
by Lindsay Camp

Morris MacMillipede – the Toast of Brussels Sprout
Mick Fitzmaurice

Mick Fitzmaurice

MORRIS MacMILLIPEDE
The Toast of Brussels Sprout

Illustrated by Satoshi Kitamura

RED FOX

A Red Fox Book

Published by Random House Children's Books
20 Vauxhall Bridge Road, London SW1V 2SA

A division of Random House UK Ltd
London Melbourne Sydney Auckland
Johannesburg and agencies throughout the world

Text © 1994 by Mick Fitzmaurice
Illustrations © 1994 by Satoshi Kitamura

1 3 5 7 9 10 8 6 4 2

First published by Andersen Press Limited 1994

Red Fox edition 1996

Printed and bound in Great Britain by
Cox & Wyman Ltd, Reading, Berkshire

RANDOM HOUSE UK Limited Reg. No. 954009

Papers used by Random House UK Limited
are natural, recyclable products made from wood grown in
sustainable forests. The manufacturing processes conform to
the environmental regulations of the country of origin

ISBN 0 09 942781 8

1

Morris Macmillipede is eight years old and has 42 pairs of legs. And 42 pairs of feet. And 42 pairs of trainers.

His mother, Millicent Macmillipede, reads the Nine O'Clock News on Bee Bee Bee Television. His father, Mackintosh M. Macmillipede, is a policeman. He arrested the Ghastly Greenfly Gang and the Big Bad Bed Bug Brothers. Thanks to Mackintosh M., they're safely locked up in Woodworm Scrubs prison.

The Macmillipedes live at 26, Rhubarb Road in Brussels Sprout, the biggest insect city in Bell Lane Market. They have a four-bedroomed house made entirely of cabbage leaves. The problem is, they love the taste of cabbage, and they're forever nibbling at the walls and floors and ceilings. Mackintosh M. is always patching up holes to stop the rain coming in.

2

Brussels Sprout is a wonderful place for a young millipede. There are playgrounds with celery slides and radish roundabouts, and lovely, smelly gutters everywhere. On Saturdays, everyone goes to watch Earwig Rovers, the champions of the Football League.

But you'll never find Morris at the football match or playing with the other boys. For Morris has a secret.

It all started when he went with his school to see the Royal Insect Ballet. His friends were bored, but Morris

loved the theatre and the dancing and the costumes and the romantic music of Flykovsky. And most of all, he loved the ballerina, Dame Gossamer Spider.

'She's so beautiful,' he sighed, 'I wish I could share her web.'

Ever since that day, he's wanted to be a ballet dancer. He hasn't told his friends or his brothers, for he knows they'd laugh at him. But when the other boys go out to play, Morris stays at home and dances with his reflection in the mirror.

3

But Morris had to tell *someone* about his dream or he'd explode. He decided to tell his mother; surely she wouldn't laugh? But Mrs Macmillipede *did* laugh.

'A ballet dancer!' she said. 'Whatever will you think of next?' She shook Morris's head to make sure his brain wasn't broken, then laughed all the way downstairs to cook the dinner.

A tear rolled down Morris's cheek and fell onto the carpet. His dream would never come true; he'd never dance with Dame Gossamer. If his own mother laughed at him, who would take him seriously?

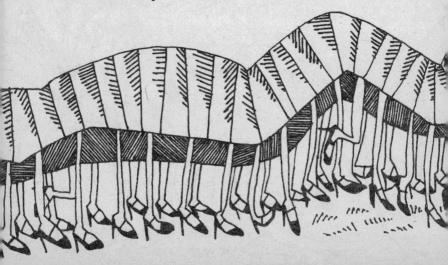

4

Morris crept out of his house and wandered sadly through the streets of Brussels Sprout. The afternoon slipped by and the sky grew dark. The Money Spiders went home from their offices, rushing to catch their trains.

'Stocks and shares,' they said to each other. 'Stocks and shares.'

Morris shivered as the icy wind sliced through his thin pullover. He was hungry, but all he had in his pocket was a piece of beetroot-flavoured bubblegum. He sat on a wall and chewed until the gum was soft and tasteless. Then he blew a broken-hearted little bubble.

Would his mother have missed him yet, he wondered? He felt so sad and lonely, he burst into tears.

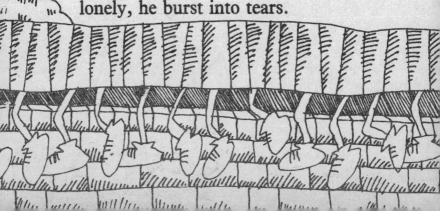

5

'Well!' said a gruff voice. 'You *do* seem sorry for yourself.'

Morris looked up. There stood an old Stag Beetle with a long, grey beard.

'If you were me,' sniffed Morris, 'you'd feel sorry too.'

'And why's that?' asked the old man, puffing at his pipe.

'Well . . .' Morris began, then told him all about his broken dream.

'Most unusual,' said the Stag Beetle when Morris had finished. 'Most boys want to play for Earwig Rovers or the England Crickets team. All the young

Beetles want to be pop stars. But you want to be a ballet dancer.'

'Yes,' said Morris in a small voice, hoping the old man wouldn't laugh. And he didn't.

'If you want to do something badly enough,' said the Beetle, 'you shouldn't care what other people think. And if at first you don't succeed, what must you do?'

'Try and try and try again,' Morris whispered.

'Quite right,' said the Beetle. Then he puffed once more at his pipe and shuffled away into the darkness.

6

By the time Morris arrived home, he was feeling much happier. He *wouldn't* care what people thought; he *would* try and try and try again.

He had a tasty tea of stale sprouts and squashed tomato, then lay on his bed thinking. Somehow he had to pay for ballet shoes and dancing lessons; but there was nothing in his money-box except a mouldy piece of chocolate.

What could he do? He stared sadly at his wallpaper with its rows of round, blue turnips. Then suddenly he had an idea. Round . . . paper . . . It was such a good idea that he set his alarm for five o'clock, nestled his 84 feet on his 84 hot-water bottles and fell fast asleep.

7

At five o'clock next morning, Morris
dragged himself out of bed. It was dark
and cold, and last night's wonderful
idea didn't seem so wonderful now.
But he wasn't going to give up.

He put on four pullovers and ran
along Rhubarb Road to Mr O'Wasp's
newsagent's shop. He'd seen the notice
in the window yesterday.

SMART BOY OR GIRL WANTED FOR NEWSPAPER ROUND

Morris pushed open the door. It was
lovely and warm inside.

'If it izzzzn't young Morrizzzz,'
buzzed Mr O'Wasp. 'And what can I
do for you?'

'I'd like a job,' said Morris.

8

He began work the next morning at half past five. It was damp and misty, and the bag of newspapers felt almost as heavy as himself. But he didn't complain; he just trudged round Brussels Sprout delivering *The News of the Worm* and *The Daily Snail*, thinking about Dame Gossamer.

It all seemed worthwhile on Saturday when Mr O'Wasp put ten pound coins into his hand. 'Here are your wagezzzzz,' he buzzed, and Morris ran home and put the money in an old

biscuit tin under his bed.

In the months that followed, Morris often wanted to turn over and go back to sleep when his alarm clock went off. But he'd reach under the bed and feel the biscuit tin growing heavier and heavier, and he'd drag himself out into the cold streets once again.

On New Year's Eve, he decided it was time to count his savings. He tipped the coins onto his carpet . . . there was £120. It was enough! Tomorrow he'd go shopping!

9

Clutching the biscuit tin, Morris pressed his nose against the shop window. His eyes were wide with excitement as he stared, not at toy soldiers or train sets, but at a row of dainty, pink ballet shoes.

He pushed open the heavy door and went inside. Dark, wooden shelves rose to the ceiling; faded photographs of ballet dancers crowded the walls. Everything in the shop seemed old, not least the owner, a Great-Great-Grand-Daddy Long Legs, who shuffled slowly from the back room.

'Can I help you?' he wheezed, looking at Morris over his gold-rimmed spectacles.

'I'd like 42 pairs of ballet shoes, please,' said Morris.

'That's enough for a whole school!' exclaimed the old man.

'But they're all for me,' said Morris, pointing to his 84 feet.

The Great-Great-Grand-Daddy Long Legs counted out the shoes.

'There, young man. That'll be £84.'

Morris gave him the money, then ran home and went straight upstairs to his bedroom. It took ages to tie up all the laces, but finally he was ready. He looked at himself in the mirror and could hardly believe what he saw.

'Morris Macmillipede,' he whispered proudly, 'you're a real ballet dancer now.'

10

The Ballet School stood halfway along
Onion Avenue. Morris went nervously
inside and found a door marked

MADAME BUTTERFLY

He pushed open the door. Madame
Butterfly lay on a sofa dressed in
flowing silks of red and blue and yellow.

'I'd like to join your ballet class,' said
Morris timidly.

'Well!' she said. 'A millipede in a
ballet class! Whatever next!'

For a moment, Morris thought she
might be laughing at him; but she took
his money seriously and sent him off to
get changed.

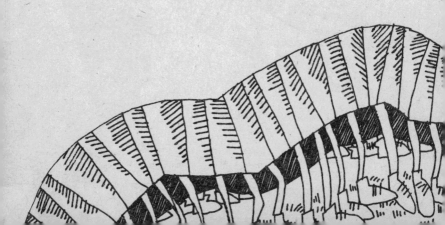

11

When he pushed open the changing room door, the other children stopped talking and stared at him. Melanie Mayfly tugged her pigtails.

'What are *you* doing here?' she sneered. 'Millipedes can't dance.'

Everyone laughed, and Morris wanted to run back home. But he bit his lip and opened his eyes wide to stop himself crying. Then he began to lace up his shoes.

'What a slow-coach!' teased Melanie Mayfly. 'The lesson will be finished before he's even dressed.'

She stuck out her tongue at Morris

and fluttered across to the mirror.

'Oh, aren't I pretty?' she sighed.

By the time Morris had put on four pairs of shoes, the others were ready, and they ran out of the changing room leaving him quite alone. He heard music; the lesson was starting without him, and he had 38 pairs of laces still to tie.

He tried to hurry, but his fingers wouldn't go any faster; they just got caught up in the knots. It was nearly half an hour before he was ready and he tiptoed timidly into the hall to join the class.

12

The hall was high and wide, and all the walls were covered with mirrors. The children stood in lines facing Madame Butterfly, who sat at a very grand piano.

'You're late!' she snapped when Morris came in. But before he could explain about all the laces, she turned back to the class.

'Let me see you jump,' she said.

Morris stared in dismay as the children leapt gracefully into the air, hovered on their wings, then landed gently on the floor. He'd *never* be able to do that. But he remembered the old Stag Beetle's words and tried his best. He jumped with his back end; he jumped with his front end; he jumped with his middle. But he couldn't jump with all of himself at once. It seemed that millipedes simply weren't designed for jumping.

'You'll have to do better than that,' sighed Madame Butterfly.

But Morris couldn't do better. If only
he had wings! If only he didn't have
so many legs! It was a terrible start –
but worse was to follow.

'Now let me see your spins,' said
Madame Butterfly.

The children stood on one leg,
fluttered their wings and spun round
in perfect circles. It wasn't even worth
Morris trying.

He hung his head and crept out of
the hall. He'd never come back, and
his heart would never stop aching.

13

But that night, Morris dreamed of the old Stag Beetle and woke up feeling ashamed that he'd given up so easily. He *would* go back. He *would* try and try and try again. Let them laugh if they wanted to.

And he *did* go back. Oh, the other children giggled; Madame Butterfly sighed and snapped. But Morris took no notice. Each week he tried his hardest, and although he was still clumsy, he improved a little every time. And in the end, even Melanie Mayfly grew bored with laughing and left him alone.

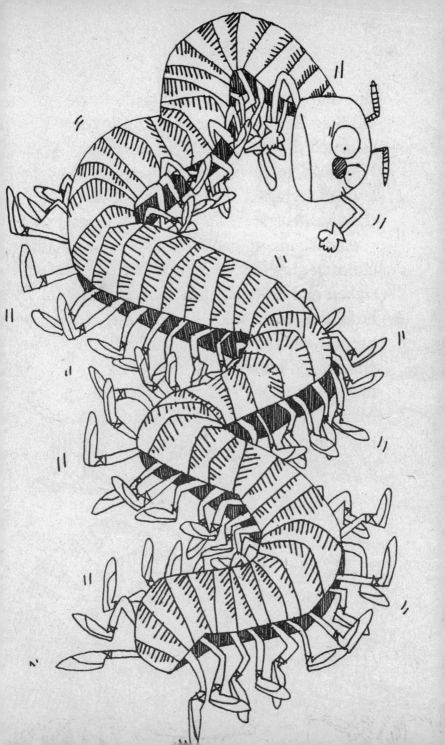

14

'Our Easter Concert is in four weeks' time,' said Madame Butterfly one day. 'We will be performing "The Sleeping Beauty". What a wonderful story! The Ugly Caterpillar sleeps in a cocoon for a hundred days, then turns into the Beautiful Butterfly.'

Melanie Mayfly was to be the Beautiful Butterfly, of course, and Martin Moth was to be the handsome Prince. Everyone else was given a part – everyone except Morris. As the others chattered excitedly, he coiled up sadly on his own in a corner. He'd tried so hard, but he wasn't good enough.

Madame Butterfly felt sorry for him. He was the worst pupil she'd ever had. But perhaps . . .

'Morris!' she called. 'Come here. I have a part for you. I want you to be the Ugly Caterpillar.'

15

Morris's part was small but very important. He had to spin across the stage into a huge silk cocoon; then Melanie Mayfly spun out of the other side as the Beautiful Butterfly. It was very difficult, and always made him dizzy. But he practised and practised until he could just about manage it.

Mrs Macmillipede made his Ugly Caterpillar costume, and all his family and friends bought tickets. As the concert drew near, Morris was so excited he couldn't concentrate at school. He was always in trouble with his teacher, Miss Louse.

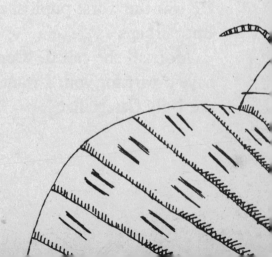

16

Finally, the great day arrived. The lights in the hall went down; the audience fell silent; Madame Butterfly played the first notes on the piano; then the curtain rose and Martin Moth began the ballet.

Half an hour later, they reached the great moment when Morris had to spin into the cocoon. Madame Butterfly played loud and fast, and Morris spun out onto the stage. Everything went perfectly, and as he approached the cocoon, he began to think of the applause he'd soon receive. But that was a terrible mistake, for he stopped thinking about spinning. His front end began to spin faster than his back end, and his long, clumsy body coiled up like a spring.

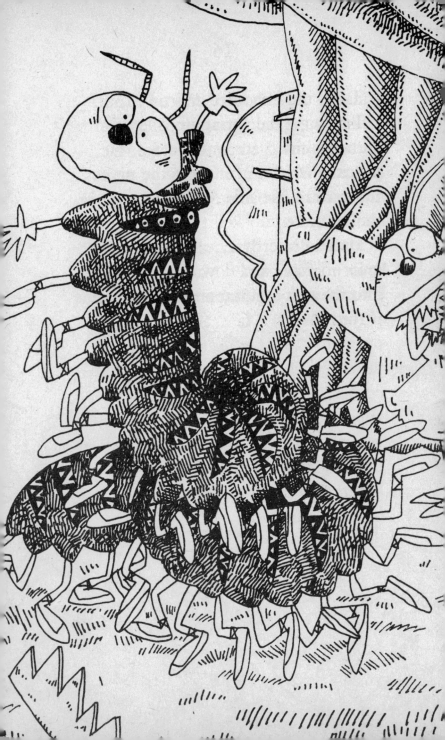

'Look out!' shouted Martin Moth.

Too late. The spring uncoiled and Morris whirled across the stage. He knocked Martin Moth into the piano; he knocked Melanie Mayfly into the audience; he knocked the scenery onto Madame Butterfly's head. Then he spun off stage and down the corridor, landing with a bump on the front steps of the school.

17

Morris had bruises everywhere, and his head wouldn't stop spinning. But the worst thing of all was the noise coming from inside – laughter. He'd made a fool of himself yet again.

He hurried away from the school and didn't stop until he reached the River Trickle. Leaning over Carrot Bridge, he stared down into the dark water. He was so miserable, he felt like throwing himself in. But he threw in his ballet shoes instead, all 42 pairs of them. They floated away into the night, taking Morris's dreams with them.

'Now, young man,' said a gruff voice. There was the old Stag Beetle, puffing away at his pipe. 'Tell me what happened.'

Morris told him the whole, sad story. 'So you see, I really did try and try and try again.'

'Indeed you did,' agreed the Beetle. 'But you see, my boy, millipedes just aren't made for ballet dancing. They have far too many legs.'

Morris felt cross; if that was the case, why had the old man encouraged him?

'But now I know you don't give up easily, I'll tell you what millipedes *are* made for,' said the Beetle.

Then he leaned over and whispered something in Morris's ear, so quietly you can't hear what he said. But it made Morris so happy, he clapped his hands and danced a jig round and round the old man.

18

Next evening, Morris went out after tea and came back two hours later with a great big grin on his face. When his mother asked him where he'd been, he just said, 'You'll see.' And he said the same thing every Thursday evening for the next six months.

One day, he came home and unrolled a bright yellow poster.

'What on earth are you up to?' asked his father.

'Just come and watch,' said Morris.

'The last time we came to watch you,' said his mother, 'you were the laughing stock of Brussels Sprout.'

But his parents agreed to come. And his brothers and all his friends bought tickets – they didn't want to miss Morris making a fool of himself again.

19

It was Saturday September 30th. The Macmillipedes drove to the theatre in their Ford Banana. What a crowd there was, all come to see Morris, all expecting to laugh at him.

At eight o'clock, the lights in the theatre went down, the curtain rose, and there in a spotlight stood Morris, wearing a top hat and tails. What would he do?

The conductor raised his arms, the orchestra set off at a tremendous pace, and Morris began to . . . TAP DANCE!

Tap tap tap went his left foot. T-t-t-t-t-tap went his right. T-t-t-t-t-t-t-tap. T-t-t-t-t-t-t-tap. T-t-t-t-t-t-t-t-t-t-t-t-t-t-tap. T-t-tap. T-t-tap. T-t-t-t-t-t-t-t-t-t-t-t-t-t-t-t-t-t-t-t-t-t-t-t-t-t-t-TAP.

The violinists' fingers flew; the pianist wished he had a hundred hands. But none of them could keep up with Morris the Miracle Macmillipede.

At the end of the show, the audience
clapped and cheered and threw
flowers. And best of all, not one person
in the whole theatre laughed.

20

There was a tremendous party in Morris's dressing-room that night; everyone wanted to be there to congratulate him.

'Well done!' said the old Stag Beetle. 'You really did try and try and try again.'

'I owe it all to you,' said Morris, giving the old man a hug.

'You owe it to all those legs of yours,' smiled the Beetle.

Morris's brothers and friends could hardly believe what had happened.

'We came to laugh,' they said. 'But we ended up cheering.'

Madame Butterfly kissed him on both cheeks.

'Darling!' she breathed. 'Didn't I always say you'd be a famous dancer one day?'

And Morris was feeling far too happy to remind her what she'd *really* said.

21

Next morning, the newspapers were full of photographs of Morris, and the phone didn't stop ringing all day. Every theatre in the country wanted him to appear. Each time he danced, he was a huge success, and he was soon known as Morris Macmillipede, the Toast of Brussels Sprout. He was as rich as a bluebottle, and he bought a house in Celery Hills where all the famous stars live.

Nothing could have made him any happier. Or so he thought, until the day the telephone rang.

'Hello,' said Morris.

'Oh, Mr Macmillipede, this is the Orange Crate Theatre. Dame Gossamer Spider is about to begin rehearsals for a new ballet, which has a most important part for a tap dancer. We were wondering . . .'

Other great reads from **Red Fox**

Further Red Fox titles that you might enjoy reading are listed on the following pages. They are available in bookshops or they can be ordered directly from us.

If you would like to order books, please send this form and the money due to:

ARROW BOOKS, BOOKSERVICE BY POST, PO BOX 29, DOUGLAS, ISLE OF MAN, BRITISH ISLES. Please enclose a cheque or postal order made out to Arrow Books Ltd for the amount due, plus 75p per book for postage and packing to a maximum of £7.50, both for orders within the UK. For customers outside the UK, please allow £1.00 per book.

NAME_____

ADDRESS_____

_____

Please print clearly.

Whilst every effort is made to keep prices low, it is sometimes necessary to increase cover prices at short notice. If you are ordering books by post, to save delay it is advisable to phone to confirm the correct price. The number to ring is THE SALES DEPARTMENT 0171 (if outside London) 973 9000.

OTHER TITLES YOU MAY ENJOY FROM RED FOX

☐ The Seven Treasure Hunts	Betsy Byars	£2.50
☐ Flossie Teacake's Fur Coat	Hunter Davies	£2.99
☐ The House that Sailed Away	Pat Hutchins	£2.99
☐ Rats!	Pat Hutchins	£2.99
☐ Burping Bertha	Michael Rosen	£2.50
☐ Who's Afraid of the Evil Eye?	Hazel Townson	£2.50
☐ Lenny and Jake Adventures	Hazel Townson	£2.99

PRICES AND OTHER DETAILS ARE LIABLE TO CHANGE

ARROW BOOKS, BOOKSERVICE BY POST, PO BOX 29, DOUGLAS, ISLE OF MAN, BRITISH ISLES

NAME...

ADDRESS ....

....

....

Please enclose a cheque or postal order made out to B.S.B.P. Ltd. for the amount due and allow the following for postage and packing:

U.K. CUSTOMERS: Please allow 75p per book to a maximum of £7.50

B.F.P.O. & EIRE: Please allow 75p per book to a maximum of £7.50

OVERSEAS CUSTOMERS: Please allow £1.00 per book.

While every effort is made to keep prices low it is sometimes necessary to increase cover prices at short notice. Arrow Books reserve the right to show new retail prices on covers which may differ from those previously advertised in the text or elsewhere.

Other great reads ❦ *from* **Red Fox**

Have a bundle of fun with the wonderful Pat Hutchins

Pat Hutchins' stories are full of wild adventure and packed with outrageous humour for younger readers to enjoy.

FOLLOW THAT BUS

A school party visit to a farm ends in chaotic comedy when two robbers steal the school bus.

ISBN 0 09 993220 2   £2.99

THE HOUSE THAT SAILED AWAY

An hilarious story of a family afloat, in their house, in the Pacific Ocean. No matter what adventures arrive, Gran always has a way to deal with them.

ISBN 0 09 993200 8   £2.99

RATS!

Sam's ploys to persuade his parents to let him have a pet rat eventually meet with success, and with Nibbles in the house, life is never the same again.

ISBN 0 09 993190 7   £2.50

Other great reads from **Red Fox**

Enjoy Jean Ure's stories of school and home life.

JO IN THE MIDDLE

The first of the popular Peter High series. When Jo starts at her new school, she determines never again to be plain, ordinary Jo-in-the-middle.

ISBN 0 09 997730 3   £2.99

FAT LOLLIPOP

The second in the Peter High series. When Jo is invited to join the Laing Gang, she's thrilled – but she also feels guilty because it means she's taking Fat Lollipop's place.

ISBN 0 09 997740 0   £2.99

A BOTTLED CHERRY ANGEL

A story of everyday school life – and the secrets that lurk beneath the surface.

ISBN 0 09 951370 6   £1.99

FRANKIE'S DAD

Frankie can't believe it when her mum marries horrible Billie Small and she has to go and live with him and his weedy son, Jasper. If only her real dad would come and rescue her . . .

ISBN 0 09 959720 9   £1.99

YOU TWO

A classroom story about being best friends – and the troubles it can bring before you find the right friend.

ISBN 0 09 938310 1   £1.95

Join the RED FOX Reader's Club

The Red Fox Reader's Club is for readers of all ages. All you have to do is ask your local bookseller or librarian for a Red Fox Reader's Club card. As an official Red Fox Reader you only have to borrow or buy eight Red Fox books in order to qualify for your own Red Fox Reader's Clubpack – full of exciting surprises! If you have any difficulty obtaining a Red Fox Reader's Club card please write to: Random House Children's Books Marketing Department, 20 Vauxhall Bridge Road, London SW1V 2SA.